A NOTE TO PARENTS

Congratulations on choosing the best in educational materials for your child. By selecting top-quality McGraw-Hill products, you can be assured that the concepts used in our books will reinforce and enhance the skills that are being taught in classrooms nationwide.

And what better way to get young readers excited than with Mercer Mayer's Little Critter, a character loved by children everywhere? Our First Readers offer simple and engaging stories about Little Critter that children can read on their own. Each level incorporates reading skills, colorful illustrations, and challenging activities.

Level 1 – The stories are simple and use repetitive language. Illustrations are highly supportive.
Level 2 - The stories begin to grow in complexity. Language is still repetitive, but it is mixed with more challenging vocabulary.
Level 3 - The stories are more complex. Sentences are longer and more varied.

To help your child make the most of this book, look at the first few pictures in the story and discuss what is happening. Ask your child to predict where the story is going. Then, once your child has read the story, have him or her review the word list and do the activities. This will reinforce vocabulary words from the story and build reading comprehension.

You are your child's first and most influential teacher. No one knows your child the way you do. Tailor your time together to reinforce a newly acquired skill or to overcome a temporary stumbling block. Praise your child delight in his or her imagination, your time together!

D1021551

Library of Congress Cataloging-in-Publication Data

Mayer, Mercer, 1943-
    Our park / by Mercer Mayer.
        p. cm. — (First readers, skills and practice)
    Summary: When Little Critter and his friends clean up their favorite park, they learn the value of hard
work and caring for the environment. Includes activities.
    ISBN 1-57768-807-4
            [1. Litter (Trash) Fiction.] I. Title. II. Series.

PZ7.M462 Ov 2001
[E] dc21   2001026598

McGraw-Hill
Children's Publishing

*A Division of The **McGraw·Hill** Companies*

Send all inquiries to:
McGraw-Hill Children's Publishing
8787 Orion Place
Columbus, OH 43240-4027

Printed in the United States of America.

1-57768-807-4

    4 5 6 7 8 9 10 PHXBK 06 05 04 03 02

 A Big Tuna Trading Company, LLC/J. R. Sansevere Book

FIRST READERS

Level 2   Grades K - 1

OUR PARK

by Mercer Mayer

McGraw-Hill
Children's Publishing

Columbus, Ohio

This is my park.
I wish it were clean.

This is our stream.
There are cans in the stream.
We can pick up the cans.

This is our playground.
There is trash on the playground.
We can pick up the trash.

9

This is our bench.
There is paper under the bench.
We can pick up the paper.

11

12

This is our picnic table.
There is garbage around
the picnic table.
We can pick up the garbage.

This is our ball field.
We can make sure it is clean, too.

14

This is our park.
We can keep it clean.

TRASH

Word Lists

Read each word in the lists below. Then, find each word in the story. Now, make up a new sentence using the word. Say your sentence out loud.

Words I Know	Challenge Words
park	clean
cans	stream
bench	playground
paper	trash
table	picnic
ball	garbage
	field

ABC Order

abcdefghijklmnopqrstuvwxyz

Write each set of words in abc order. Look at the first letter in each word to help you.

clean   _____

around   _____

bench   _____

trash   _____

stream   _____

park   _____

19

Word Fun

Read the questions below. Write your answers on the blanks on the next page. The first one has been done for you. Use the Word List below to help you.

1. What did Little Critter and his friends clean first?

2. What did they pick up from the playground?

3. What was around the picnic table?

4. What was the paper under?

5. Where did Little Critter meet his friends?

6. What did they find in the stream?

Word List

bench   park

cans   stream

garbage   trash

1. <u>s</u> <u>t</u> <u>r</u> <u>e</u> <u>a</u> <u>m</u>

2. ___ ___ ___ ___ ___

3. ___ ___ ___ ___ ___ ___

4. ___ ___ ___ ___ ___

5. ___ ___ ___ ___

6. ___ ___ ___ ___

What did the park ranger say to Little Critter and his friends? To find out, read the letters in the box from top to bottom.

21

Make a Sign

Let's make a sign so people will remember to clean up at your park or playground.

Here are some tips:

1. Use a large piece of paper or posterboard.

2. Use large letters.

3. Use a dark crayon or marker.

4. Keep your message simple and positive.

5. Decorate your sign.

Try phrases like:

1. Please pick up your trash.

2. Please keep our park clean.

Use this page to practice making a sign.

Answer Key

page 19
ABC Order

clean	around
around	bench
bench	clean

trash	park
stream	stream
park	trash

page 21
Word Fun

1. s t r e a m
2. t r a s h
3. g a r b a g e
4. b e n c h
5. p a r k
6. c a n s

page 23
Make a Sign

Answers will vary.